Have You Seen This Chameleon?

Leon the chameleon is missing! But ace detective
Private I. Guana is on the case. He searches high
(through the forest) and low (through the swamp),
questioning bullfrogs and salamanders and tacking
up posters (showing Leon in a variety of colors,
of course) along the way – until he unexpectedly
stumbles across the solution to the mystery.

"Humorously bold illustrations perfectly complement
the tongue-in-cheek telling of this exciting story."
   –American Bookseller, Pick of the Lists

For my father.

I. Guana and I also want to thank Red,
whose lizards are truly an inspiration.

©1995 by Nina Laden.
Book design by Cathleen O'Brien.
Typeset in Old Typewriter Regular and Alternate.
The illustrations in this books were rendered in pastels.
Printed in Hong Kong

Library of Congress Cataloging-in-Publication Data
Laden, Nina.
Private I. Guana : the case of the missing chameleon
/ by Nina Laden.
p.   cm.
Summary : Private I. Guana is hired to
search the forest for Leon, a missing chameleon.
ISBN: 0-8118-0940-4 (HB); ISBN: 0-8118-2463-2 (PB)
1. Iguanas-Fiction.   2. Chameleons-Fiction.
3. Mystery and detective stories.
4. Humorous stories.   I. Title.
PZ7.L13735Pr   1995
Fic -dc20   95-2828   CIP   AC

Distributed in Canada by Raincoast Books
8680 Cambie Street, Vancouver, B.C. V6P 6M9

10 9 8 7 6 5 4 3 2 1

Chronicle Books
85 Second Street, San Francisco, California 94105
www.chroniclebooks.com/Kids

PRIVATE I. GUANA

The Case of the Missing Chameleon

by Nina Laden

Chronicle Books
San Francisco

I was sitting at my desk when I got the call. "Private I. Guana here," I said. "Yes, I can find missing lizards. A chameleon? Well . . . okay. Why don't you come over to my office. And bring a photo." As I hung up, I wondered if I should have said okay. Chameleons are hard to find. But she sounded upset. I guess I'm a sucker for a lizard in distress.

"**YOU** can call me Liz," she said as she made herself comfortable in my office. "Here is a recent snapshot of Leon. He didn't come home for dinner one night last week. I had made his favorite, cricket stew . . . I haven't seen him since. He was acting a little strange, changing colors every minute. He's always been the stay-at-home type, and well, frankly . . . boring. I'm afraid he could be in trouble." I puffed myself up and said, "Now, don't you worry, Liz. If I can't find Leon, no one can. By the way," I asked, "what color was he when you last saw him?"

Quickly I made a pile of posters of Leon, the missing chameleon. Not knowing what color he was, I figured I'd color each poster differently. Too bad Leon didn't have a scar, or a tattoo. Then I set out to hang them up wherever I could. I stopped first to check in with Officer Croaker, the bullfrog chief of police. Officer Croaker, who had a habit of jumping to conclusions, said, "A missing chameleon? That's a waste of time. Probably pretending to be a rock." I said, "Thanks for your help, Officer. Maybe I'll go talk to some boulders."

So I hit the dirt to see what I could dig up. I plastered the forest with posters. I went over fields, under rocks, and up trees. I talked to turtles, lizards, snakes, frogs, toads, and a couple of skinks. It was getting dark. My feet were tired, my tongue was tied, and I had no clues, no tales, no trails, no Leon. Maybe this chameleon had really disappeared for good. But maybe I just wasn't looking in the right place.

I decided to head
home and start again in the
morning. On the way, I saw a
firefly-like glow in the distance
by the swamp. I had forgotten
all about The Lizard Lounge.
It was kind of a slimy place,
where only the most cold-blooded
reptiles hung out. My head
was telling me not to go there.
But my stomach said, "Boy, I
sure could go for some of
those greasy fried grasshoppers
and a tall cold drink." So I
put my stomach in charge and
followed it.

The Lizard Lounge was buzzing with activity. I scoped out the place, making sure not to ruffle any feathers or step on any tails. I made my way to the back and sat at a table where I could keep an eye on things. The menu was my first order of business. I noticed that the special this week was cricket stew. "It's probably just a coincidence," I thought to myself.

A sweet salamander sashayed over to my table. "I'm Sally, your waitress," she said. "What's a nice amphibian like you doing in a place like this?" I asked her. When I didn't get an answer, I ordered my food. I noticed a sign on the stage that said, This week: Camille and the Gila Girls I said, "Hey Sally, who's this Camille?" Sally smiled. "I don't know who Camille is. She just appeared out of the blue a few days ago, but boy, can she sing. She fits right in with our house band, the Gila Girls. You really should stay for the show."

I had nothing better to do, and the fried grasshoppers were pretty tasty, so I decided to stay. Soon the place got dark. Everyone stopped what they were doing. All eyes were on the stage. The Gila Girls took their places. Then a spotlight came on. The curtain rustled, and out slithered the most unusual chameleon I had ever seen. Something about her was familiar. It was like I'd seen her face somewhere before. I tried to remember, but then she started to sing, and my mind went blank. I was hypnotized.

When the show was over,
Camille bowed and disappeared
behind the curtain. I clapped
and whistled as loud as I
could. There was no doubt I
had just seen a star. I had
to get an autograph. Maybe
it was instinct. Maybe I was
crazy. But here I was, sneaking
around backstage at The Lizard
Lounge, looking for her dressing
room door.

I was so nervous, I was shaking. I knocked on her door, and when a voice said, "Yes? Come in," I nearly shed my skin. I couldn't believe I was alone with an amazing singer. I stammered, "Ca-Camille, I-I wanted to get your autograph . . . could you sign this?" And I pulled out the first thing I could find from my pocket and handed it to her.

Camille looked shocked. She said, "How did you know?" What did I know? I wondered. I was totally confused. Then I put two and two together. I knew there was something familiar about Camille. By mistake, I had handed her the photo of Leon to sign. And then I realized that Camille was Leon, the missing chameleon.

I had hit the jackpot. "You know Liz is looking for you," I said. "She's very upset. She misses you." Leon took off his wig and sighed. "I miss her, too. But I was worried Liz thought I was too boring. I thought she might leave me for someone more exciting. I wanted to show her that I had talent, that I could be somebody special--maybe even a star! When I heard that the Gila Girls needed a new singer, I jumped at the chance to polish my act. Naturally, I blended right in."

And so I closed the case of the missing Camille/Leon. Last I heard, Leon was the singing sensation of the swamp. Liz watches the show and then returns to the kitchen, where she's the new head chef. Her cricket stew is getting rave reviews. It seems that the The Lizard Lounge is actually becoming a respectable place. As for me, who knows what the next case will bring? A frog that jumped bail . . . a turtle running a shell game . . . a poisoned snake . . . just remember, if you've got a problem, give me a call. The name is Private I. Guana. The "I" stands for "I'll be waiting."

A GUIDE TO USING THIS BOOK

Private I. Guana can be used to inspire discussions about storytelling, giving and receiving clues, and wordplay. As the book is read aloud, allow time for everyone to look closely at the illustrations. After a complete reading, go back to the beginning and discuss the story page by page. Children will enjoy the humor found both in the words and illustrations.

A NOTE FROM NINA LADEN ON WRITING THIS BOOK

I am often asked where I got the idea for this book. Initially, I was inspired by old detective movies. I imagined a place called The Lizard Lounge. Then one day, I put a few words together – private eye and iguana and I came up with a character name – Private I. Guana. I had a setting, and a character, but I didn't have a story. I knew that Private I. Guana had to solve a case, but what case? Then I thought about different reptiles. Chameleons intrigued me because they could blend in with their surroundings. If a chameleon were missing, it would be hard to find. That was my story. Private I. Guana: The Case of the Missing Chameleon.

DISCUSSION TOPICS

- What does a detective do? What is a mystery? What are clues? How are mysteries solved?

- What is a disguise? Why does Private I. Guana suspect Leon might be disguised so no one will find him?

- Private I. Guana searches in both the forest and swamp to find the missing chameleon. What types of animals live in the forest? The swamp? What is a reptile? How many different types of reptiles can you find in the story?

- Private I. Guana is a detective. What other jobs do the characters hold in this story? What kinds of jobs do the people you know have?

- Imagine you are telling this story. How would you change your voice to sound like a detective, or Camille singing? What happens if you lower your voice to tell the story? Raise your voice?

- In this story, Leon pretends to be someone else. Think of things people do to change their appearance. What are they? When someone changes his or her appearance, does it make you think of anything new about that person?